Rush

Of

Many

Waters

Also by Pauly Hart

Rush of Many Waters:

Volume Eight

By Pauly Hart

ISBN: 978-1-955399-12-8
Library of Congress Catalog Data is available at: Loc.gov
This book is available at cost on Amazon.com and wherever
fine books are sold.
Front Cover Art by Franz Marc:
Front cover design by Pauly Hart
Paperback version printed in Savannah, Georgia, USA,
where available.
First Edition, 2021
Author Contact: EmpiresAndGenerals@gmail.com
Author Website: PaulyHart.com

Contents

The Night Eyed

The Setup

They called them "The Night Eyed" and they were a little less friendly than your average mountain folk. Most of the time you could catch them up above the tree line, clamoring on the scree on all fours like the cats people thought they were. But they weren't cats at all. Not even close.

Being stationed at the Polebridge Ranger Station most of the week, I kept a sharp eye out for them, even from my house up near Demers Ridge. You could see them every full moon out screaming and hollering - having a good old time. But you had to get used to the sounds. The first time people heard 'em, they thought someone was getting murdered.

It was April 20th, 2019 when everything went down. I had to write the very same report up for the State Police, so you're getting the retelling of the story… Except… I don't think anyone's going to believe me… In the official report I had to be pretty vague about some details. Hopefully in this version, I can get some things cleared up that I didn't really want to include in the "official story."

Anyway, if I know the state police at all, they're just going to write my story off as "night terrors" or something, even though I haven't had that since I was six years old. Whatever. I'm not scared of anything. All that got beat out of me in the Marine Corp. You could send me up after those crazy people with a machete and I'd be alright. But no one is going to do that, because they don't even think they exist. I've got their "official press release" about the night eyed.

They ignore the issue altogether. They called them Pumas and were done with it. Well they weren't Pumas, not even close. Pumas, Mountain Lions, Cougars, Catamounts - its all the same animal. America's largest cat. Scary as all get out. The Puma were all over these parts. As an employee of the DNR, its part of my job description to make sure each adult Puma is accounted for. We use drones to investigate new litters, and whenever we have a newborn death, we tally it. We even have names for 'em. It's a lot of work, especially when we have to go tag-and-release, when the populations are low.

Now east, up in the Lewis Range, the Glacial National Park DNR has everything reckoned out. So many tourists come up there the state has them on point. But west of the Livingston Ridge, down in our valley, things are a different matter. Our action comes from the west. The Flathead County Sheriff's department and the Forestry Service both get up here from time to time, mostly to handle drunken loggers, or find lost tourists, or poachers… But it's me up here all the time. They think they know what goes on, but they might as well be tourists themselves.

Down the middle of the valley runs North Fork Flathead River. It runs from Flathead Canada into Flathead National Forest, then dumps into Flathead Lake. All this sits on the Northside of the Indian Reservation. Guess which tribe it is? Yes, genius, the Flatheads.

The Beginning

It was cold and wet and I hadn't brought my snowshoes, but the blood trail led right up into it. That sucked, because I could see the fur tufts and knew what I was looking for and it wasn't an animal. It was one of the night eyed folk, and I knew it. The fur was from a black bear, you could see fur every now and again, and there were four sets of prints from our hunters, leading, pulling, pushing, and dragging the bear up and over the drifts. Their feet and hands left the usual markings, long skinny human feet, splayed toes and hands. More instinctive creatures than anything else. I wonder what it was that had made them want to hunt the bear? They couldn't be that hungry, could they?

From what I had been reading about gorillas, the main two big boys ate mostly fruits or vegetables. Humans had the same type of teeth, and the lowland and mountain gorilla ate only 3% animal life. The rest of the time, they were vegetarians. That's the key to health, I think, mimic nature when I can, and get technology to help you along into the progression of the human animal. There are no termites here, so my gorilla mimic can't be perfect, but… Hey. How does roast beef sound?

But I wouldn't eat a bear. They taste disgusting. Why would you kill a bear? They didn't need the meat. There were plenty of mice and rabbits to eat that they could catch. And they did just that, let me tell you, I've picked

through enough scat to know. It's kinda funny seeing the tiny bones, but...
To each their own, eh?

I pulled up my GPS and marked the spot. Then I took some photos and packed everything back up. I might not be able to make it back up this way again for a while, so I suppose my curiosity would have to do it. Before I left, I found a nice clearing and spray painted a huge orange "X" on the rock. I maybe could get back here with my biggest drone.

I was walking back down as a pack of them were coming up. As I measured it, about six hundred meters down from where I had abandoned the trail, there they were, coming right up towards me. Four of them - a family unit. The wind was flowing across the slope, the prevailing winds are west by southwest this time of year, making hunting a little easier, but also stuff like this can happen as well if you're headed south east and your prey is coming the opposite direction. No one moved... Well... My right hand lost its glove and found my side-arm, but after that, no one moved.

I had seen a lot of the night eyed in the past. I had photos of them with my drone, and I even had 'em named. There were around twenty four of them in the pack that I was familiar with, and the four that stood in front of me, I didn't recognize.

The Confrontation

Instead of the gun, maybe I should have gone for the candy bars. The whole situation might have come out a little differently, maybe. The four that stood in front of me were men, their markings over their head and groin areas were more pronounced than that of the females. The one in front had a balding head, and many scars on his arms and shoulders. He was the one who stood erect and addressed me, hands in the air, pawing, like a trained house cat.

"Awch aw arroaa..." was as far as he got before another male from behind him pushed him away and moved in front to address me. This one wasn't the friendly sort and bared his teeth and began howling. As he did so, the other three sort of submitted and began the intimidation dance to match suit. They were very slowly fanning out around me, trying to make a net to capture and kill me.

Fuckin A.

My .357 held seven shots. The first one went through the head of the leader and created a red, gray, and black splash on the tree behind him. As he was leaning towards me, facing up the hill, the force of the impact brought him up fully perpendicular to the ground, and then in an almost slow motion effect, he fell backwards into the snow... The echo of the report rolled through down the slope and slowly brought back ghost echoes from in and around the area.

Fuckin A.

A shot from a .357 does a lot to a very quiet morning. I hadn't noticed the sounds of the chipmunk and grackle and various other wildlife that surrounded me, but after a gunshot, when everything is quiet, you sure notice the silence. It lasted for the eternity of 45 seconds until a hawk broke the silence with a *"creeeee"* and one of them made a dash for me. Two in the chest. He's down. I didn't want to wait so I just blasted the other two before they could come at me. I had emptied all the rounds.

Fuckin A.

I got the speed loader from my belt and chambered up the next batch of bullets as quick as I could. I was a bit deaf, but I could tell that all was quiet except for the old one. He lay on his back. I had punctured his lung and the wheezing was rattling his chest every time he inhaled. He was crying, looking at me, with an outstretched arm.

"Awch aw arroaa..." I knelt beside him with my bowie knife and put it in his hand and helped him bring it into his throat. The questions in his eyes died with him.

Fuckin A.

The Chase

It was a three hour walk to my Jeep Commander, and it was an hour drive back to the station. The drive wasn't what worried me. It was getting the hell out of Dodge that was my main concern. I didn't know how close the rest of the tribe was. I didn't want to find out. I needed to go, and go very, very quickly. The group of four had between them a bag of some sorts. I had grabbed it before scrambling down the mountain at pell-mell speed. I wondered what was in the bag. Coming to a small ledge of rock, I stopped and opened it up. What in the world could they have been lugging along?

It was a caribou skin bag and it contained some odds and ends. Bones mostly. Two skulls most importantly. Smaller and slimmer than humans but not animals at all. This must be some of their tribe. Incredible. No one had ever seen anything like this before. I would be abso-fuckinlutely famous. I took them and stuffed them into my backpack. It was then that I heard the screams.

Normally when I hear them, I'm up alone in my station, and I can go investigate in the morning. But being this close, it sent chills up my spine. Fuck, that was close. I needed to move, move, move. I had my pack back on and was turning to leave when a glint caught my eye. Inside the pack, almost at the bottom was something shiny. I reached in. A flint knife of intricate design lay in my hand. Leather and wood over a full tang of flint and a very sharp little number of a blade, polished to a shine. It was gorgeous and it went in my left cargo pocket.

Another scream. I needed to beat feet. Without movement, they would catch me. Like an idiot, I hopped down from the rock and scrambled... And lost my footing. I'm a dumbass. I fell, tumbled, and fell some more, sliding along the scree. The ledge after the outcropping was sharper than I had figured, which may have been a vital mistake. Like. Literally, my vitality might drop to zero. Oh, and I was still falling, scrambling, and, yes, another two or three tumbles. Thanks to the tree that stopped me, but no thanks to the rock that rushed up and knocked me out.

The sun was too low when I came to and I was concussed. I knew I was concussed because the second time I vomited, I was super dizzy. Ugh. This is no good. My left leg was screaming at me as well. Great. Now I've only got one leg and I still have to hoof it out of here before crazy mountain people eat my face. Well, they probably wouldn't eat my face first. They might save that for later and add it to one of their skull collections. Who the fuck knew? I didn't, and I didn't want to find out either. I tried standing on my leg....

Fuckin A.

Sitting down was so much nicer, but nothing that I had time for. Sitting, I shimmied my pants down and my thermals to check out my... Ugly yellow left knee. Oh man, I must have hyper-extended it or twisted it or something... Fuck. I must have been out for longer than thirty minutes for it to already look this bad.

I took off my neck-wrap and double wrapped it around the knee, cinching it tight. Holding back the yelps and whimpers, I wiped the tears from my eyes and pulled my pants back up. It didn't make it any more comfortable, but the tightness would do me some good. I knew this was going to suck hardcore, but I had time to heal after I survived. Right now, making sure my hunters were not captors was the most pressing item on my mind.

I took some deer trails and one or two man-made trails. I was a little lost but had a general idea of where I was. My head hurt like a mo-fo. I needed to go a little to my South and I should be back on track. The sound of rushing water threw me off, but I kept running anyway. When I came upon the little lake, I knew that I was more lost than I had thought. My back was drenched with sweat. I had abandoned my toque long ago, it had just been too warm to wear it. Trail running was a sport all of its own, and I, the one legged man, was overdressed for it.

I got out my GPS and powered it up. Parke Creek should be right to my west. I had never even seen this landscape before. Where in the world was I? North of Reuter Peak? Holy shit. Had I been running the wrong way? How concussed was I? The sun would set soon and I was nowhere near where I thought I was. I hadn't heard their screams for a while now, but that didn't mean anything. When they hunted, they were well-coordinated and often ran in silence, as long as they could see each other.

In the glen where I was, the sun was already behind the ridge, and here in the valley it was already getting dark. As much as it might be the death of me, I had to make camp. You can't run in the mountains at night, no matter who you are. I would just have to stay awake.

The Camp

Stopping and camping probably seems like foolishness to a city person. I don't know who you are or where you hail from, but I know the forest and I will give you some information that will help you better understand where I am coming from.

In the forest, the dark is darker than it is in the city, even in the farmlands. If you have ever been "camping" in the woods, even in the middle of the day, you can find places where the sun doesn't reach you. And in the middle of the night, in these same places, the moon and stars can't reach you either. In cities and towns, and even in farm-land, you have something called: "light-pollution." It's the effect of man-made light against the night sky. Out near, let's say, Billings Montana, you have to go almost twenty miles out of town to get back to an "almost natural" state. Even a hundred miles out, there's sometimes a .0011 effect of light pollution.

Out here, it was a zero. That's 0.00. No light. And there were no stars. And there was no moon. It was so black that often you couldn't see your hand in front of your face. Day-hiking was a perilous adventure if you didn't know what you were doing. Even people like me, who had done it all their life, and even sometimes twisted their ankle, it's rough... And that's when you can see everything. A one legged man does not travel fast... In the daylight, or at any time. A one legged man is often a dead man.

So when you're camping, at any time during the year, you need to find a good place to do it. You had to have access to, or bring with you, a good supply of water. If you were going to survive for longer than a day, you needed water.

In survival, always remember the rules of three. To maintain a healthy body, you need oxygen every three minutes, you need water every three hours, you need food every three days, and you need shelter every three days. In the mountains, in the dark, you need hope every three minutes. Raw survival and healthy survival are different. In raw survival, certain things change. Water can be up to three days, food up to three weeks, and shelter (unless you're wet) can be up to three weeks... But hope... Hope you need every three seconds.

And here we get to the subject of fire. Fire gives you hope. Fire gives you warmth. Fire gives you light. Fire gives you a place to boil your water. Fire gives you a place to cook. Fire scares away wildlife. Fire scares away mosquitoes. Fire gives you a fixed point of navigation. Fire is good... Usually. In this instance, fire would give away my position to them who hunted me... And that would be a bad thing. I had to go without fire.

After gathering some pine branches and building a small lean-to against a straight back wall, a distance away from the lake, I set about cleaning the site. This is a skill that I've developed over time. Most city folk tromp through an area and leave traces of themselves everywhere. They never see what they've done to nature, but I was alright at it.

It was already dark.

There was nothing left to do but wait.

The Capture

"Having done all to stand, stand therefore." Nana would say to me right before we got ready to walk in the front door of her church. And there I was, hair slicked back with her saliva, sporting a blue bow-tie and my tiny powder blue checkered vest, waiting for Sunday school to start. After Sunday school, would be the main service. The sweaty preacher waiving his Bible around, greasy hair flapping in his face, asking if there were any sinners that needed repenting. He was in my face now, on the first row, his eyes looking into mine - nose to nose. His breath smelled like the forest.

Rough hands grabbed me and forced me to my feet. His gray hair was dripping with sweat. Eyes piercing into mine with electric blue. He shook me by the collar and shoulders. He grabbed my bag away from me and threw me to the ground again where I fell with a splash. Were these the tears of the saints? There must have been a lot of repenting going on. I could hear the crashing and banging of many lost souls giving their lives to Jesus right then and there. It must have been Palm Sunday. Branches were everywhere.

Then there were five preachers, with five Bibles. They were lifting me up and tying my hands, moving me roughly. Carrying me out. Carrying me down the aisle to get some repenting. Their feet had no shoes on them and the mud came up from between their toes. Thunder rolled. Or was that the organ playing? "Softly and tenderly Jesus is calling... Calling for you and for me... BOOM... Thunder rolled again and the preachers laughed at me. They had yellow sharpened teeth and blue tattoos on their faces.

I was concussed.

Fuckin A.

These weren't preachers at all.

The Death

The one legged man sat alone in a cave. No, that's not right. The one legged man died alone in a cave. Yeah. That's better. The one legged man woke up and then died. How awful. But what a fitting end to this story. Because that's exactly what happened. I died.

In case you're wondering. It was a long and horrible death. My leg eventually healed, and I think that's the only reason that they kept me around for as long as they did. It was soon after that they started eating me bit by bit. I don't think that I was a great tasting meat, but they seemed to enjoy causing me pain. With no food, I had little energy to fight them, and they took off the bottom half of my right leg first and made some sort of soup with the foot. Well... Not so much a soup, as a jelly.

They would cauterize the cut each time to make sure I didn't bleed out. With the top part of that leg, a week later, they had a bit more trouble. They ended up pulling my leg out of my hip and sort of working their way around the wound with a hot knife. I can only remember the fire and the pain.

With the first leg gone, they did a little less to keep me prisoner, and when they took my other leg, they didn't guard me at all. They allowed me to eat from the common area, and I might have eaten some of my own flesh, but hunger did weird things to me. When my arms were gone, they did not feed me at all.

The final day came when they stood over me and crushed my throat. Then the world turned black and I was dead.

The Rescue

I don't know how long I had been at the camp, but it must have been a couple of days or so because I was still alive. I hadn't been kidnapped and eaten... Just the kidnapping part had happened. The only thing that was true about any of that was that it was raining and I was almost drowning. The cliff I had built my quick lean-to under was a waterfall and it was coming down on me, pounding me down into the mud, drowning me. If it had been much earlier, I may have drowned. I had to get up and get out of this. And that was no easy doing.

Pulling myself up involved a lot of rolling to the side and getting my legs unstuck. My left leg had a dull ache to it, but otherwise seemed alright. Getting out of the rain was the first priority, before I drowned or froze to death. I was already shivering. It was pitch black, and the rain didn't help me not seeing anything. I found what should be my hat with my hand, and, wet as it was, squashed it down on my head. It might do a little to keep me warm at least.

A couple more rolls and I was free from the muck. I felt my bag at my side so I grabbed it and tried to stand. *OUCH* my leg was still not okay and I almost went down. But I could hobble my way out of here, and if that was what it took, then so be it. Down the mountain side, clutching at this and that. I could just barely make out the trees as they were coming up in front of me, so that's how I went. Blurry tree to blurry tree to tree downward. Thank God it wasn't too steep, I had good footing. Wait. Did I just thank God?

Fuckin A.

Why not? I had nothing to lose.

"God! If you can hear me! Let me live!" I cried at the top of my lungs.

If I had been out for only hours, the night eyed would still be on me. If I had been out for days, then they had given up on me and left me to the elements. At this temperature, I didn't have long.

"God! If you're there, let me know!" I screamed again.

"How did you know my name was Bob?" a voice hollered back through the rain.

The Next Day

Bob Cooper was a volunteer fireman who helped work the odd crisis every now and again. He had shone his flashlight in my eyes and led me back down to the road, where he and other volunteers had been looking for me for five days. Five days was a long time in the mountains and I had been out for almost all of it, in a state of delirium, under my lean-to. I was famished and ate a Whatchamacallit candy bar while they radioed the rest of the team.

"You're lucky you called my name," Bob said, face smiling from the front seat. His grin was the most beautiful thing I had ever seen. "I was just getting ready to head back down and go home."

"Yeah." I said. "Thanks."

But I hadn't called Bob's name. I had prayed. And that prayer was answered. By some miracle or coincidence, I didn't know.

Laying in the hospital bed, getting checked out, it was nice to be warm and dry. My boss had come by to check on me and ask me what had happened. "Panthers" I said. "Gonna get some sleep. Talk to you in the morning." I rolled over, and he left.

Rick Sanchez over at Mountain View Mennonite was there when I arrived the next morning. Didn't really even know they had Mexican Mennonites, but, whatever. I had left the hospital without checking out because I needed to see if a church fella knew what it was that happened. If God answered my prayers maybe there was something to it. Maybe Nana had been right all along. Rick said he was only a deacon there but he would answer my questions all the same. I gave him the whole story.

"Oh you mean the Tepeyollotl." he said, eyeing me funny. "Yeah we know about them. They got here long before the white man did, and they'll probably be here long after we're gone."

I showed him the skulls that somehow, miraculously were still in my bag and he gave a low whistle.

He looked it over very slowly, fingers going over the cheek bones gingerly.

"You got two of them?" he asked earnestly.

"Right here." I handed the other one to him.

"Hold on, I'll be right back." he said, and walked to the back office of the church. What, is he going to get a camera or something?

But he never came back.

As I limped to the front door of the church and opened it up, his black Denali was kicking up dust, turning left and driving down the street. "Fuckin A." I said to myself. "Now who's gonna believe me?"

Leaving you

As the old man looked around, he wondered what had changed in his life to bring him to this place. He saw neither friend nor enemy here, but he wondered what would have happened if he had the power to turn back time. The power to change it all. The power to heal.

The night was as black as any other evening, and Dean wandered thru the neighborhood with no purpose. It was not his neighborhood, but it was not far away from his. As a matter of fact, it was only three blocks down, but Dean like to take his path here when he made his way to the park. He walked the park around this time in the day, on the average of once a week, depending on the work schedule. There was nothing interesting on this block as there was on any other, but for the scores of happy families that usually came home around this time every day.

On some days he would not see as many families as others, but on the average, he was able to catch at least two to three of them arriving, spilling happily out of their mini-vans and SUV's and romping into the house. Mothers carrying groceries, Mothers picking up children from school with arm loads of groceries. He liked the sounds and the sites of it all. he missed it and yearned for it again in his own life.

It had been three years ago when he had left his own family and travelled to Durst, Oklahoma. He had left them in Cincinnati all alone.

He never knew fully why he did it. There were times in his thinking that he could explain the inexplicable feelings that were there and could reason that there were a thousand valid points to his departure. But of course there were other times where he thought that he had been crazy then and was still crazy for never going back to his estranged wife and three children in Ohio.

She often called, asking how he was, and he sent regular support, even though she said that she did not need it, she still cashed the checks. He had not talked to the children since that day, but she assured him that they were fine and they sent their regards.

They sent their regards. What a statement. The truth was that they were an emotional wreckage, all three. They had never gotten over what he had done to them and perhaps they never would. Jackie had a boyfriend now and though he loved the children, the kids saw thru him and accepted the substitute as one who was drowning, awaiting rescue by something larger than a plank of wood.

He had reached the park, lost in thought. There were no children yet, but there would be, playing on the plastic lumber construction that made up the playground.

"Those things sure have changed from when I was young." He thought to himself.

Back when he had been a youngster, they were all hard metal and sometimes, if you went to a better part of town, you could find one of the wooden fort-style playsets. those were a blast, and sometimes they even had a tire-swing.

He sat at a bench, lost in thought. Around him, squirrels scampered, afraid of him at first, but then regaining courage, came poking around for scraps of bread. Durst was a strange place where the wild animals weren't really wild, but the teenagers made up for it. Fortunately there were none of them loitering at the park today. they made him ill-at-ease, reminding him of his own wasted youth.

In the distance, thunder boomed.

Of Thieving

The Dread Fiend Marmoset took hope at the coming sun. Lightinger had done a splendid job that night and it was time that he put the trusted sword away. The night watchman he had killed had only left behind his cloak and a pile of coins amidst the black smoke.

Lightinger hummed as it went into the scabbard. Such swords only grew in power, not diminished, and each time the pain of controlling it grew greater. The Dread Fiend Marmoset looked at his hand. Blue and welting and painful. He put on his gloves. That would do for a while until he could dress his hand properly. He pulled out his treasure. All intact and to his liking. Everything was fine, except for his hand, and that would be remedied shortly. The Dread Fiend Marmoset picked up himself, and his bag of loot and crept along the rooftops of the quiet metropolis of Three-State.

Eighteen, Nineteen, Twenty blocks later he dropped down to the streets. He would have gone faster and farther, but people were beginning to wake from their merry weekend festivities and start their morning routines. The morning bell had tolled and was waking the city slowly but surely. Changing clothes in less than eight seconds was always one of the most exhilarating and challenging parts of the getaway, but it was also one of the most dangerous. Having your entire plan become vulnerable to a changeover of any kind was hazardous.

Marmoset held the gold in his hand, and eyed the merchandise on the counter. Normally he would have scoffed at the trade, but he was in a hurry, and the Fors family would soon be on his heels for the ransacking of their villa. They had somehow (majik he suspected) known that it was him that had robbed them. And he needed to make good his escape.

"Forty-two?" he asked again.

"That's the brunt of it, yes." The husky and ill-kept barterman looked at him with his one good eye. Marmoset had woken the trader up, but suspected that he looked this way on an everyday basis. The days where beggars could not be choosers was upon the now hapless thief, and the barterman, although still groggy, was alert enough to know it.

"Very well. Peace be with you." Marmoset said. A flick of the wrist and the gold disappeared up his sleeve. He was out the door before the barterman had a chance to say farewell.

The streets were still cold. Marmoset could feel them underneath his slim shoes. Good for hiking? No. For scaling walls? Yes. He might need to do both, but these shoes would be the better pick. He reached around the third corner and picked up a small black purse that he had left only minutes before entering in on the trader's shop. "Damn bartermen. They have nothing better to do that to pick on me..."

The bell interrupted him. Instinct took over. The sunrise bell had gone off not long before. There should be no bell now. He was in the next ally to his left. Hop, hop, leap. Rooftop. He fastened the purse around him. Silence after three tolls. Then a short toll! He had been found out!

Lightinger's vengeance would have to wait. Right now he had to put distance between himself and anyone who would try and capture him. He noticed a shadow with the Fors emblem on the streets below. *There shouldn't be any guards yet!* He thought. Had the barterman tipped them off?

The arrow that entered his head was quite the answer to that. As he fell off the roof he knew he was done. The bad news was it was going to hurt when he landed. The good news was, whoever had just killed him would know the power of revenge. Lightinger had a way of making itself known wherever it went. The Fors guard would mix his soul with those already trapped in his sword.

Lightinger clattered to the ground amidst some clothes and a purse in a puff of black smoke. The guard kicked the clothes, wondering where the thief had gone. No matter. He would turn in the purse and claim the reward, but this sword would be the prize for him. He pulled it out of the scabbard and peered at the blade.

The Dread Fiend Marmoset peered back. He might just betray the man the same way that he had been betrayed. It would be delicious. But first he had to deal with all the souls trapped in the sword. In order to control its destiny, he would have to become its ruler. And there were many to overcome.

Poems

Only Friend

Lives linger
Senses tingle
I feel your rain again

Somedays you shine
Brighter than life
Somedays you weep for me

Visions will drift off
Spirits will lift off
I feel your rain again

Rainbows will cheer me
But none come as dear me
You are my only friend

Rainbows will cheer me
But none come as dear me
You are my only friend

Rainbows will cheer me
But none come as dear me
You are my only friend

We are voices

We are voices
whispering, screaming.
Nameless voices,

crying out for love.
Listlessly, relentlessly,
dexterously climbing,
treading the surface,
wanting the out pour.
Breathe on us...
we cry at night.
Heal our land,
we face our fright.
We are the voices
whispering, dying,
treading the surface.
Breathe on us...
we cry, we cry.

Everything You Meant

everything i was
everywhere i was going
all i wanted
was your crush
and freedom meant
all inside your love

for the wonder
and the splendor
in each caress
and each brush
of your supple lips
on my neck

supple lips
moistened tits
tender kiss
dreamers bliss
vampire tongue

heart undone
sandwich love
cripples crush

in futile ways you
played me the viola
i bent and whined
while you stroked
and plucked me
my tender heart
so generously lost

and now i flounder
so lost at the sea
dark and stormy
under purple skies
i cry day and night
for a beacon

supple lips
moistened tits
tender kiss
dreamers bliss
vampire tongue
heart undone
sandwich love
cripples crush

greener II
(happiness where you should be)
-prompted by Grant Campbell

said one goat to the cow
"i shall travel there one day"
and lived his life on

said one hermit to the vagabond
"i shall make my mark yet"
and lived his life on

said the president to the country
"i shall never tell a lie"
and lived his life on

said God to a world
"i shall soon come again"
and did as He said,
but they weren't ready just yet.

said a people to the Deity
"come back in a month"
and got left for the bugs.

they should have been ready.
they could have prepared.
happiness where they should be.
hell where they are.

Soulfood

Passed the alter
into the soulfood
by the lifting of hands
by the blood of the lamb
past the laver
into the soulfood
towards the painted gates
by the word of our testimony
passed the courts
into the soulfood
away from the thieves den

and not loving my life
passed the table
into the soulfood
closer to the holy place
by the word of the Lord
Past the doorway
into the soulfood
to the holiest of holies
by the spirit of truth
passed the old life
into the soulfood
yes, my lord
into your heart.

Nothing

Pretense meant nothing to me

when I looked into her eyes

Gazing into coolness

matching spy for spy

She read my like a Bible

Chapter, book, and verse

All the words dried on my tongue

all the lines rehearsed

Pretense meant nothing

as I looked into her eyes

All I could do was think of love

and moments passed us by

ode to skylight coffeehouse

oh coffeeshop the beautiful
oh coffeeshop the drinks
oh lovely old place
to kick up my feet

if ever the latte
if ever the vibe
i would take up my shelter
and call you my tribe

i love this old place
it's stolen my heart
if ever i left you
i would fall apart

while i type and ponder
of what this all means
i whiff the aroma
of freshly ground beans

I remember

I remember Erin and Ted.
I remember Fletch and Alex.
I remember Roxanne and Wesley.
I remember Dawn and Bill.

I remember Colin and Dulce'.
I remember James and Dennis.
I remember Sarah and Christian.
I remember Adam and Travis.
I remember Alice and Susan.
I remember Lisa and Jason.
I remember Sammy and Missy.
I remember Nyleen and Christian.
I remember Joy and Nealy.
I remember a cloudy day.
I remember tears rolling down my cheeks.
I remember waving goodbye as you drove off.
I remember seeing your note.
I remember my brother Tim.
I remember the black and blue eye.
I remember Lonnie and Ted.
I remember the look on their faces.
I remember regret and secret love.
I remember Monopoly and forgiveness.
I remember something I forgot.
I remember loss.
I remember friends.
I remember you.

Essays

Drew Allen

Drew Allen is a contemporary Artist who specializes in surreal expressionism and who dabbles in realism, abstract, and very mixed media visual fine art. He is about my age and I.Q. and shares my unique world-view that life is weird people are nuts and bugs are great. Anyone who believes that these things are prerequisite of life paradigm is sure to be a good pal of mine. So I met Drew one afternoon around three and one half years ago at his art studio/gallery in mid-town Tulsa, Oklahoma. He was in the middle of a meeting with several people discussing the ins and outs of a play called Heartdance. The play was in the beginning steps of becoming professional and the people in the room were mainly musicians who were being brought on board to help put the sound track together. Several people I already knew form the Tulsa scene including Garo Nargiz, a worship leader for a really cool church called the bible fellowship. After Hello's all around I was invited to join them. I said "Hi, I'm supposed to meet Drew Allen, Dan Amerine sent me over."

Drew: "I'm Drew, what do you need?"

Me: "Well Dan said that you needed musicians, but I mostly just write poetry."

Ruth: "Well take a seat, Welcome."

Aha! Ruth, she invited me in to join them.

Me: "Oh, Okay thanks. What exactly are you guys working on? Oh! Hi Garo."

Garo: "Hey Pauly..."

Ruth: "You know each other?" we nodded.

Drew: "From where?"

Me: "From OBF. I used to go there before I moved back from Indiana."

Drew: "Wow!"

Ruth: "Well, small world. Have a seat why don't you?"

And so it goes. Heartdance, I came to find out was a brainchild of Ruth Ketchums. It told the story of Christ form a mid 90s street gang mentality.

Ruth: "Its kind of an analogy told thru the eyes of a street gang. Joshua comes to save them but they kill him."

Pretty much Joshua being Jesus and I guess the street gang would be every one else. A cool story that has transmogrified thru the years and has developed into an amazing play, of which I became a part of because good old Dan Amerine sent me on a quest to meet Drew. And my life was forever changed.

As a recent arrival (Again) to Tulsa, I was unfortunately living with my father at his house with my mother- in- law Linda. Beautiful people to be sure, but I was unnecessarily taxing their love with my stay. Dan had told me that he could talk to his landlord about living with him and his roommate Noah Branum in Broken Arrow, a suburb of Tulsa. Now I had for a time worked in Broken Arrow at the movies & as an usher and had found the town quaint, but confusing because of their inability to keep the names of Tulsa streets the same name. 81st street became Olive or 145th became St. Louis or some nonsense like that very trite and unwelcome competition to Tulsa's sprawling metropolis area. I'm sure that thousands agree that this was a poor decision but the town stuck to its guns and left it be. So I moved in anyway with Dan and Noah. Jeff Davenport was the house owner and rented to single Christian men, of whom I was one. No Crack, no prostitutes, no spitting, etc… great rules for wholesome living. My worst habits at the time were promiscuity and smoking. Well, smoking cigarettes. I tried pot for a while and found that it was a worthless habit. So I was stuck with Joe Camel.

The end of the meeting came to a close and I found myself volunteering my free time to help Ruth write a song for a character named Boo- Dog. The song spoke remorse and regret at his choosing a life of crime in the play and it ended up a great rock ballad never to be recorded. Ruth cast Boo-Dog as a "Playah" and not as a "Rockah". Rap would have been more to her liking. But no fretting involved I signed up with them anyway. The other thing that came from the meeting was (much more to the importance of myself and m future) meeting with Drew Allen to discuss my volunteering to just 'hang out' at the studio. Up till this point my life has been typified by the lyrics from a <u>Third eye blind</u> song: "An angry boy, a but too insane…" But things were going to change for the better; I just couldn't see it yet.

My first time hanging out with Drew went off without a hitch. I came over after morning in with Dan and Noah to kill time. Drew's place was right off the corner of 31st and Yale a block away from a seedy strip club called "Cloud-Nine." Believe me I've never been inside of that place, but there was noting dreamy about the whole institution. Passing by there everyday almost causes me to weep at the poor women's choice of employment. But around the corner was my own hang out.

Drew showed me around the place and told me what he did. He painted. Paint was everywhere. I was covering canvases that covered almost every room in the place. He painted clouds, he painted " Color Voyages", he painted tulips, and he painted on taxidermy shark. The left (or Western) part of the building was completely sold to finish works, whereas the right (or eastern) half of the building was split up between his studio, his stepmother's studio and the dead files office of his father's insurance company. His step- mother* worked primarily on mosaics and was pretty famous for her works.

*Linda Allen. I found the whole processing fascinating. The tour, the person, and the fact that someone out there was making real money at this completely blew me away. I was hooked, lined, and beached by this guy.

The next week or two I came over around three times. I was a waiter at Rib Crib and it was your typical Barbeque joint. Located everywhere in the Tulsa area I worked at the only one with a liquor bar at 81st and Yale. Swanky in many ways* it was primarily built by Brett Chandler (the owner) as a franchise show-off. Every Saturday morning they would train all the Rib Crib employees there who were going to work at other stores. I guess you could say it was the Flag Ship store. Oh my third day there I waited on the owner's wife and didn't get fired, so I must have been okay at the job. I made money and it was nice, but it wasn't my passion. My passion was the studio and all it meant. I got to watch drew work one day and it was exhilarating. He was not your typical painter. Dressed only in some ripped up shorts with paint in his hair he answered his door with...

"Oh, hey. Come on in, but I'm in the "ZONE" so if you wanna hang out don't say anything. And left me in the foyer with a "Lock the door when you come back!"

Okay, I saw genius in action. Bottles and buckets, caulk, painting knives and paper plates for a pallet, he spread is soul onto a 48x60 in. canvas. This was nuts, but intriguing. Crawling on the floor around the prostate art-to-be, he splattered, mixed, spread, shaped, and molded a cloud formation into something alive and real. I don't know how much time went by but soon there was the offer to get a bite to eat. To me, this meant Wendy's down the street, but for Drew it was an invitation for a quick snack in the kitchen. Wendy's won. My treat, my car, and the dollar menu.

Sitting there then I recollect my second impression of the man. He seemed almost post orgasmic after his "Zone-High" from painting. I did not fully feel it from painting but have experienced before from poetry. When it turns out just like you planned you...well, you can't explain it. So I became a painter at heart that moment and later that decision would manifest itself.

At Wendy's that day, I also learned something else of Drew. As a father of four from two separate women he had many an opportunity to go nut. And instead of throwing his hands up in the air and giving up, because "Nuts" was evil and wrong, he embraced it and used it to fuel his work. I also learned of his faith. Faith to me used to be a system of belief patterns that shaped your inner ethos that colored your view of the universe and life. Faith was turning out to be shaky and unforgiving and ever so deceitful. Religion was not faith, but at this time I did not know that.

Drew's faith like mine had developed through an experience of hardship. His faith was in a wild and passionate creator who was in love with his children and all of their craziness, whereas mine was stoic and logical. I believed that God loved me, Drew's was insane and complete rebuttal to all of the training. I had gone thru the years ago, again, in Tulsa, Oklahoma.

Where was this guy all my life? Would meeting him earlier have caused me less grief in my Christianity? Who knows? No. Who cares? Better. I have found to not live in the "What-ifs" of this life and concentrate on the "What-now's."

Three junior bacon cheeseburgers later, I had gotten to the heart of the matter. I needed what Drew was and I was wondering if he would help me find it and if he had a problem sharing more of who he was with me. "No problem." was the response.

Finally… Someone to look up to.

Cemetery or Seminary

When I finally arrived at "Bible School" I had a firm grasp on what I thought was a very biblical worldview. I knew the hard basics of who Israel was, the basic tenets of Christ and his teachings, and had some small degree of success working in my local church. I had some pretty finicky theological points but the major hardwiring had already been set in concrete in my deepest ethos. It would take four years of busying myself with American Churchianity to understand that I was living a false Christianity. It was a real religion and it had some very good teachings, and it was even based in the Bible, but… *BUT* it was not Christianity… Not pure Christianity at least. And that's what hurt the most.

In Bible School we learned a lot. A whole lot of the Bible, this and that and a little bit of over here and some from over there… Just enough to wash over the entire Bible without getting too detailed. It was a Charismatic school so a lot of the teaching I received was about: "Health and Wealth" and other things of that nature in modern Charismania. It wasn't that horrible except that it was persistent. If I got sick then there was something wrong with my faith. If I was poor then I wasn't praying hard enough. On and on. A little bit of revelation overemphasized leads quickly into heresy. Oh that's a cool statement. You can take that one home with you. Wait. Paul already said it: "A little leaven thickens the whole lump." Soon enough, I was just as lump-headed as the rest of them. Jesus never got sick and he always had a place to lay his head, yet, blessed are the poor.

It was Keith Wheeler who really knocked some sense into me though. He showed me how to think and act and walk like Jesus would want me to walk. He showed me what the response was to a hurting world, and he showed me the errors of mega-church building. He blew my mind open with what Christ should look like versus what Christ looked like today. And without him helping me divorce myself from the bloated gold-seeking whore that the American had become. Oh. Did I say that out loud? Yes. Churches are buildings. Christ called us the be the assembly. We were to meet in homes and to take communion with each other. We were to baptize and teach and make disciples. We weren't supposed to take tithes to pay on mortgages. But… That's another story.

Keith led me to find discernment between what I had learned, what I "knew" and what was indoctrination versus what was actual truth. He showed me that I needed to take and apply my society into the teachings of The Word, instead of trying to get The Word to fit into the confines of my society. It was a paradigm shift. To unlearn what I had learned. To find truth only in the Spirit who took up residence inside of me and to base that learning on the Bible, the Word of God. If I read something in a book, the Bible was to be the arbiter of truth for that knowledge. Did it sit firmly on the cornerstone of Christ? No? Then let it slide off because it didn't belong there to begin with. "What is truth?" Pilate asked. "I am the way, the truth, the life" Christ answers.

It took five missionary trips and four years of school to really get at the message that Keith was trying to instill in me. And it's taken my whole life to try to understand how that applies to my existence and to become everything that God wants me to be. I'm not anywhere near finished with my journey though. Maybe by the day I die I will be closer than I am now. Here's hoping. So I went back to childhood. Back to everything. What was real and what was indoctrination? What did the Bible support as good science and what was just poop? My goal was to throw out all the poop and let the truth remain. "Eat the hay and spit out the sticks" was good advice I got about a horse once. It seemed legitimate and I thought I would give it a try.

For the remainder of my time at the Seminary I kept this as a shield or a filter in front of my ears and eyes. Was what they said proven by scripture? What was good and what was bad? It was hard going at first, but I think, like the Bereans in the book of Acts, I studied everything to show myself approved for the gospel of God. And it was a close call. I barely came out on top. I was lucky to have had Keith in my life at that time. Otherwise, I might be one of those "Pork Chop Pastors" to this day.

the breakthrough

all of my life I was and have been witness to a breakthrough of Gods anointing. I have seen and witnessed many a time in my life where God would be doing something so severe and I would be at the forefront of it. There were times in my childhood that seemed inconsequential at the time, but were in fact very obvious times of Gods mighty hand upon my life.

I remember walking alone on the beach at the age of three... first having abandoned my parents to their own demise, having run away. I was way too little for such a venture, but I felt that I had things under control then. God saved me miraculously then. I was living in Indonesia at the time and could have been kidnapped and sold off for some strange sex-slave. I had blonde hair and bright blue eyes, and could have generated a lot of income for some sick minded individual.

There was a time also when I came very close to dying, and my dad saved me. I was riding the escalators (again in Indonesia) and I had fallen down right near the edge. Escalators have come a long way since then, but back then the teeth were of such magnitude that they would have chewed me up quite quickly. He scooped me up and threw me to safety just in the nick of time. Praise God!

Well, I was plagued with many a terror in my life, and i think it all culminated when i was in the summer before my senior year of high school. I had come home from working at a Christian summer camp, and had decided that if Christ was King, then he was King completely or not at all. I had an addiction to comic books, and role-playing games at the time, that sucked the very soul out of my life. I decided to burn them all and let Christ take his place on the throne of my life. It was a rather tough decision, because I could have sold them all and made a nice profit but I burned them. Quite literally. If feel that it was then that I had my breakthrough.

Breakthroughs come and go and each new conquest in your life serves as a new opportunity to see your life in a new light. I chose my moment. Jesus had waited all along for me to come to my decision, and He was there when I made it. Now I live life fuller, give God more thanks, and pretty much have a better view on life now that all my idols have been destroyed.